AN ENGINEER'S APPROACH TO RELIGION

AN ENGINEER'S APPROACH TO RELIGION

BEING BORN TOUCHES THE WORLD

Stanley E. McFarland

ReadersMagnet, LLC

An Engineer's Approach to Religion
Copyright © 2021 by Stanley E. McFarland

Published in the United States of America
ISBN Paperback: 978-1-956780-21-5
ISBN Hardback: 978-1-956780-22-2
ISBN eBook: 978-1-956780-20-8

All rights reserved. No part of this publication may be reproduced, stored in a retrieval system or transmitted in any way by any means, electronic, mechanical, photocopy, recording or otherwise without the prior permission of the author except as provided by USA copyright law.

The opinions expressed by the author are not necessarily those of ReadersMagnet, LLC.

ReadersMagnet, LLC
10620 Treena Street, Suite 230 | San Diego, California, 92131 USA
1.619.354.2643 | www.readersmagnet.com

Book design copyright © 2021 by ReadersMagnet, LLC. All rights reserved.
Cover design by Ericka Obando
Interior design by Renalie Malinao

1
INTRODUCTION

Yesterday, I watched Trump's inaugural address. And this morning, I listened to the prayer service and learned of his first actions as president was to gut Obama's health care act. I felt compelled to begin to write this paper. This paper is an attempt to explain in a rational manner how we think. I am an engineer and I have been trained to think in a certain manner. What follows is my attempt to explain this process.

In any engineering subject, the first step is to set up the logic behind what follows. In this case I am dealing with beliefs which I consider the basics of any religion. I define a belief as a decision based on insufficient data. If you say I believe in something, you don't know that something. A lot of what we say we know we have assumed we have sufficient data to make that judgment. What follows is my opinion as to what is necessary to make valid judgments.

My first step was to set up engineering axioms to deal with the subject. Those axioms are:

    1. *The truth is true and only the truth is true.*

2. *Nothing real can be threatened, nothing unreal exist.*
3. *I think therefore I am.*

What follows is in my opinion as to what has and is happening to us and how we can respond in a rational peaceful way.

Truth

When I started to work with this material, I wanted something solid and concrete to work with. I thought the truth would be a good place to start. In the process of developing this material, I found the truth to be very difficult to identify. Invariably, someone will say, "Whose truth?" I have no clear answer for this problem, but I think you will, as we developed this material, find that the answer will become evident. One of the things that you should know about the truth is that you cannot change it. This fact suggests that if you want peace, accept the truth. All conflict is derived from a misperception of the truth. If you want to eliminate conflict, search for the truth. The only thing you can do with the truth is accept it.

Test of Validity

When you talk about truths, it is helpful to have some form of test of validity. The second axiom is a test of validity for the truth. I got this phrase from The Course in Miracles. This book suggests that when you see things differently, miracles can happen. The second axiom is "Nothing real can be threatened, nothing unreal exists." This statement seems to be self-evident, but as we get into this material it is evident we do not believe it. For a thing to be real, it must exist. It must exist now, in the past, and in the future. This is not how we can currently define reality. Our culture has placed reality in the objective domain. Our culture is a materialistic culture that is primarily considered with objects and it is causing us problems.

One of the basic problems with this validity issue is all bodies die. Bodies are objects. The human brain is an object. When the brain stops functioning, the body dies. Most of us know we are real! There is that statement, "From dust thy comes, to dust thy goest," which suggests bodies are unreal. They do change form. They do lose the ability to think. Are bodies real? Are we real? What is the nature of thought? Does thinking make us real? We live our lives based on what we believe on this issue.

Objective versus Subjective

When I retired, I applied for and became a substitute teacher in the public school system. I thought I would be substituting for high school classes but I found myself in grade school classes quite often. In the lower grades, there were often discussions about objective versus subjective definitions. These definitions were part of the test the grade school kids were given and were influential in allowing these kids to pass those tests. The definition these grade school kids were given was basically what I find in the dictionary. An object is defined as a thing that can be seen or touched. An object is an existing object or fact independent of the mind. It's real. And it is concerned with the realities of things rather than the thoughts of whoever's involved. Subject, on the other hand, is defined as under the authority or control of another and subjective is defined as resulting from the feelings of the person thinking; not objective. Subjective emphasizes the ideas and feelings of those involved. The net result of this is that students are taught that objects are real and that thinking or things of the mind are unreal. Now I ask you if all objects change form and seeing and touching are forms of perception, what is real? You have heard the phrase, "Seeing is believing." Seeing is an objective phenomenon based on dictionary definition and believing is a subjective phenomenon based on dictionary definition. This phrase sets those two concepts equal to each other. What you see you have given meaning to and you've given everything you see all the meaning it has for you. If something exists out there that you have not given meaning to, you can't see it. I say you can't see what you don't believe.

I Think Therefore I Am.

"I think therefore I am" is a five-word sentence with a whole lot of meaning. In order to understand it, one needs to know who or what is "I" and what it means to think. Starting with "I," there are three possible choices. The first choice is first-person singular. People who take this position are generally egotistical. Their general philosophy is "I think therefore I am, the hell with the rest of the world." These egos are concerned about themselves and everything they do revolves around them. Most of us know people like this and in the last election we had one who ran for president. Their worldview is "me first." You can create a paradox using this philosophy by simply restating the axiom in the plural. It comes out as "we think therefore we are the rest of the world." Each of us has to resolve this paradox and it will reflect our world view.

I had difficulty in writing this presentation for the second concept of "I." A group of people can refer to themselves as I. Examples are our church, classes, corporations, political parties, etc. I kept wanting to bring in examples supporting my position that were unrelated to what happened. Hillary Clinton was a "we person." In her campaign, she kept referring to the power that we have together. She wanted to be the president for the whole country. She kept saying, "We are stronger if we do it together." She wanted us to have a national identity of "we, the people."

The third choice for "I" is God. This choice basically represents the concept that we all are one. God did not run in the election, but he was in control.

The campaign appeared to be polarizing. The election itself demonstrated just exactly how polarizing this whole process was. In my opinion, we have roughly half the

United States population following an ego and roughly half the US population following a person who believes we can solve problems together. This polarization was carried into the inaugural process by a president who said I will make this country first. A president who operates under the assumption that he is in control makes us his subjects. The cost of freedom is eternal vigilance. Under the Trump presidency, eternal vigilance is going to be an issue. The Women's March that occurred on Saturday was part of this vigilance issue. Only history will tell the outcome.

The other important word in "I think therefore I am" is "think." What does it mean to think? I choose to see "I" as God in this statement. Therefore, thinking comes from God. The thoughts of God are real. And one of the questions that need answers is do thoughts leave the mind? My sense is they do not leave the mind and therefore all thoughts come from God and are still in his mind. Now it is clear that we seem to be able to think. And the question is, are our thoughts real? This question takes us back to the discussion earlier about anything real can't be threatened, anything unreal just simply doesn't exist. Part of that definition was anything real has to exist in the past, now, and in the future. Since God is eternal, his thoughts must also be eternal and they are still in his mind therefore they are real. If we as individuals can think with God's thoughts, then our thoughts are his thoughts and they are real. This is consistent with the third axiom, which basically says, "I am real." But it's inconsistent with the idea that I am a body.

Now the question is what are God's thoughts? I have often heard that God is a God of love. He is a loving God. Therefore, his thoughts must be loving. If we think loving thoughts, we are thinking with God's thoughts. If we start to think in terms of hateful, nasty, unloving thoughts we actually stop thinking and we create illusions. Now illusions by definition are unreal, but we can believe in them. Believing in them makes them real for us. We have the power to make anything we want seem real. This is a tremendous power that we do not fully comprehend. This source of illusions is the basis for most of what follows.

2

TERMS AND DEFINITIONS

What follows is a list of terms and conditions that have bearing on what was discussed above and is part of the conclusions which will follow. I am making a list because some terms are relevant to all of what was said before and is part of my conclusions. Some terms are more specific, so rather than discuss them and make them part of the logic and the conclusions I decided to list them separately.

Attack

An attack is a thought or action designed to hurt another. It depends on one's belief that you can hurt another. It is inconsistent with the concept that we are all one. If we are one, what we do to another we do to ourselves. So, an attack on another is an attack on ourselves. This is part of what I was trying to get at from in my discussion of "I" in the second person discussed above. Hillary did not recognize the significance of the attacks on Trump. At one point, she described Trump followers in very negative terms. This was an attack on their egos and I'm sure a lot of those egos voted against Hillary and it may have cost her the election.

Evil

Evil can be defined as those choices we make that separate us from the perfection of God. Evil was first described in Genesis chapter 3 in the Bible. If you go back and read that section, you will find that Adam and Eve chose not to follow God's word and eat of the tree of knowledge of good and evil. That choice separated them from the perfection of God and allowed them to see themselves as naked and ashamed. Those are the kinds of choices we make every day. The choice to do things that are not of God's will separate us from him and they are nothing more than choices we make. They are mistakes and can be corrected.

Sin

I define sin, as a belief in something that is untrue. This allows me to use logic to deal with very emotional issues. Sin carries a lot of baggage. It is generally considered evil. And one of the questions that should be asked is, is it real? The answer is yes, if one continues to believe in something that is untrue. It is true for you! The answer is no, if you decide that what you believe needs to be changed. One of the questions that can be asked is, is it better to sin or make a mistake? The answer is making a mistake because when you make a mistake you have recognized the error and you are willing to fix it. To sin means one does not recognize it as a mistake and will continue to believe in the error.

Sincerity

Sincerity is the process of matching one's words with one's actions. This was an issue in the past campaign for the president. An ego will say anything to benefit himself I saw Trump as a colossal ego. A genius at presenting images that were consistent with the group he was speaking to. This worked fine for Trump as a candidate. I don't think this will work for Trump as president. As president, Trump needs to be perceived as sincere. This is inconsistent with Trump as a candidate. The voting public was unable to deal with this issue. Only history will tell the outcome.

Lying

I consider lying to be the process of getting someone else to believe in something that's untrue. In other words, they are trying to get you to sin. In the above discussion of sin, I treated it as a choice, a possible mistake that was correctable. Biblically to sin is to be against God. And the wages of sin are death. Lying is a deliberate attempt to get you to believe in something someone knows is not true. I consider this to be the same as an attempt to murder. Our culture is lying to us. We believe that objects are real. Our bodies are objects. And our bodies (our identities) are all dying. We need to correct this!

Eternal

Eternal is a time-based concept. The units of eternity are now. This is much different than our current unit of time which is seconds. The concept of now in our current time-based system is so short it appears not to exist. We are dealing with GIC seconds in our computer system and we have methods of measurement on the order of the billionth of a second. So, in our current culture, now just might barely exist. Some say it doesn't exist. My point here is that it takes time to learn that we are sinners. We have all eternity to make the choice to follow God's will. Time began when we decided to do things our way. Time will end when we decide to do things God's way. We have all eternity to make this decision. It's a decision we will make. Truth is an eternal concept. Reality is an eternal concept. In this world, we have chosen to see each other as separate identities and have developed illusions that allow us to exist here in time. Biblically this gets discussed as I am the alpha and omega.

Happiness

Happiness is a term that has changed over the years. Our forefathers set up a system of government that said we had certain inalienable rights. They are life, liberty, and the pursuit of happiness. Obama in one of his final speeches referenced us to those inalienable rights. But he did not define what was meant by the pursuit of happiness. I think our forefathers meant that true happiness results when we are right with God. Our country used this as a test of validity for almost two hundred years. And we had a government that, by and large, we were proud of. In recent years, happiness has changed meaning in that it now has to do with our status in life, which is largely materialistic and has to do with how much money we make. We are no longer that proud of our country. Trump continues to say, "I will make our country great again." He doesn't say how but the implications are that it has to do with our wealth and status (happiness). Happiness can be a test of validity, but it must be right with God.

Prayer

Prayer is a religious term. Most people believe in the power of prayer. For prayer to work there must be some sort of connection to each and every one of us including God. Without that connection, it simply does not work. I don't know this, but I'd like to suggest that connection is the Holy Spirit. The Holy Spirit, who knows the truth, will not interfere with what you want, but will present truthful alternates for whatever choices we make. The Holy Spirit is unobtrusive. He's always there. Some would call this our conscience. This is opposed to the ego, which sits on our shoulder and screams at us to do things that will benefit us alone. The ego knows nothing and will create illusions as long as they will benefit him. It is our choice who to follow.

Violence

Violence is the forcible change in something. Hurricanes are violent. Tornadoes are violent. Some dance routines are violent. Football games are violent. Violence can be entertaining. The problem is not violence per se but the idea that violence solves problems. When you try and solve a problem with violence, you simply create more violence. Believing that violence solves problems is untrue. In most of our violent entertainment, violence is used to show a solution to some sort of problem. This works out in governmental actions. On a personal level, it shows up as domestic violence. In other words, believing that violence solves problems is a sin. Let me give you an example.

On September 11, 2001, a small group of people came to this country believing that violence solves problems and brought down the twin towers. This was an extreme act of violence that they thought would solve some of their problems. And shortly thereafter, we as a country responded by bombing Iraq. This was also an extreme act of violence. It was a violent response to violence. Did it solve problems? Today, sixteen years later, we are still dealing with a world in which terrorism plays a major role. Is this also a violent response to violence? I have defined violence as a sin which results in death. How many people are going to have to die before we learn that violence does not solve problems? Put another way, using violence to solve problems is not a loving act.

Government

The function of government is to collectively respond to violence. The problem is that the government tends to be the biggest perpetrators of violence. In the case of 9/11, we recognized that some of the people involved in the attack came from Afghanistan. We as a country began to try and understand the people from Afghanistan. I was proud of our response. I remember seeing a picture of a woman that seemed to reflect the people of that nation. The process of understanding those people seem to be moving quite well. Our government decided to drop food packages from airplanes. This was a humane gesture and seemed to extend the desire of the American people to understand and quote "love our enemies." But things changed when someone designed a food package as a bomb. I thought we should search for the people responsible and charge them with war crimes. Instead, we wound up bombing Iraq.

On a local level, the police force is often used as the group that enforces local laws. The idea that they're there to serve and protect recognizes their legitimate purpose. But when they forcibly impose their views on minorities, they violate the concept of protect and serve. As a nation, we are currently working this issue out. There is a conflict here, but I do not feel that we have the proper guidelines to solve it. We need to know what's right and wrong.

Forgiveness

Forgiveness is a major teaching of Jesus. It is not about another. Forgiving someone of some offence does nothing to them. It does however have major effects on oneself. Seeing another as having offended you is not loving. It is the seeing that is the problem. What you do unto another you do unto yourself. Seeing another separate from God separates you from God. The trick is seeing another as a child of God. This helps you see yourself as a child of God. One cannot forgive another for something one believes as real. If it is real, it comes from God and why would one want to forgive someone for doing God's work? This takes us back to the second axiom. Forgiveness is the process of recognizing that the forgivable offence is an illusion. It is not real. It means nothing and it needs to be let go.

Beliefs

Beliefs are incredibly powerful. Beliefs have been considered part of the domain of religion. Facts have been considered the domain of science. Recently the difference between religion and science has gotten confused. Religion has its creeds. Science has its objectivity defined in part by the definition of perception which is purely subjective. Nowhere does it describe what is meant when someone says, "I believe." I think what is meant by "I believe" is "I don't know," but I am willing to work hard to make what "I don't know" true for me. Jesus said, "I am the truth and the way. I and my father are one." He says, "Believe in me."

I have the Bible on Kindle. I searched the phrase "I believe." Not once is it attributed to Jesus. I believe he knew. Keep this in mind when you read what follows.

3

ACHIEVING OUR COUNTRY

I recently read Achieving Our Country by Richard Rorry. The title closely matches what I am trying to do with this writing. Rorry is a philosophy professor who has tried to analyze our history and show how it has created our country as we know it. This process makes him, in his own terms, a spectator. I, on the other hand, am trying to show how our thoughts and changing our thoughts can change our country and that makes me an activist or a participant. I would prefer to see this writing as a guide in achieving our country. The introduction contains a list of axioms designed to be used in this process. The terms I list are concepts that can change the way we see ourselves. I deliberately left out three important concepts. They are ego, Holy Spirit, and love. I did not want to define these terms because they are intensely personal and I want the reader to freely choose to see things differently.

Rorry's first paragraph seems to fit what I'm trying to do. And I quote,

National pride is to countries what self-respect is to individuals: a necessary condition for self-improvement. Too much national pride can produce bellicosity and imperialism, just as excessive self-respect can produce arrogance. But just too little self-respect makes it difficult for a person to display moral courage, so insufficient national pride makes energetic and effective debate about national policy unlikely. Emotional involvement with one's country--feelings of intense shame or of glowing pride aroused by various parts of his history, and by various present-day national politics-is necessary if political deliberation is to be imaginative and productive. Such deliberation will probably not occur unless pride out weighs shame.

Again, I quote Rorry,

Nations rely on artist and intellectuals to create images of, and to tell stories about, the national past. Competition for political leadership is in part a competition between different stories about a nation's self-identity, and between different symbols of its greatness. In America, at the end of the twentieth century, few inspiring images and stories are being proffered.

None of this explains how we think. Again, quoting Rorry,

> Some people find American citizenship impossible and vigorous participation in electoral politics pointless. They associate American patriotism with an endorsement of the atrocities; the importation of American slaves, the slaughter of Native Americans, the rape of ancient forest, and the Vietnam War. Many of them think of national pride as appropriate only for chauvinists: for this sort of American who rejoices that Americans can still orchestrate something like the Gulf War, and still bring deadly force to bear whenever and wherever it chooses.

This seems to be a statement of how we feel rather than how we think.

Again, quoting Rorry, "American hypocrisy and self-deception is pointless unless accompanied by an effort to give American's reason to be proud of themselves in the future." Our current test of validity is happiness, where happiness means status and wealth. This leaves us with a sense of hypocrisy and wrongness, particularly when that status or well-being has been obtained at the cost of another.

Again, quoting Rorry, "For much of European and American history, nations have asked themselves how they appear in the eyes of the Christian God." For Americans, this was positive while we used happiness as our test of validity where happiness meant being right with God. According to Rorry, "Both Dewy and Whitman ... hoped that United States would be the place where a religion of love would finally replace a religion of fear."

Rorry wrote:

> We are the greatest because we put ourselves in the place of God: our existence is our existence, and our existence is in the future. Other nations thought of themselves as hints to the glory of God we redefine God is our future selves.

I find this statement disturbing because of Trump's repeated statement, "I will make this country great again." Again, according to Rorry,

> The left, the party of hope, sees our country's moral identity is still to be achieved, rather than as needing to be preserved. The right thinks that our country already has a moral identity, and hopes to keep their identity intact. It fears economic and political change, and therefore easily becomes the pawn of the rich and powerful-the people whose

selfish interest are served by forestalling such change.

At the beginning of the campaign for this last election, the issue appeared to be between the haves and the have-nots. Trump's first issue was with illegal immigrants. He appeared to blame them for our economic problems. They were criminals, they were taking our jobs, etc. He got the attention of a lot of individuals that were concerned about the status of our economy. If Trump had started his campaign with the idea that I will create an environment in which illegal immigrants will find jobs along with the rest of our economic community, I would've had an entirely different view of his sincerity and the campaign would've taken a radically different path. We elected him because of our perception of him as a candidate. With Trump as president, we need to be vigilant for our individual freedoms.

Again, according to Rorry,

> To be a moral agent is to be unable to imagine living with oneself after committing certain acts. But now suppose one has in fact done one of these things one could not have imagined doing, and finds that one is still alive.

This is another way of defining sin. I have defined sin as a choice that can be corrected. To be a moral agent, according to Rorry, sounds like hell. I don't believe in hell.

Again, according to Rorry,

> One consequence of the Vietnam War was a generation of Americans who suspected that our country was unachievable----that the war not only could never be forgiven, but has shown us to be a nation conceived in sin, and irredeemable. This suspicion lingers. As long as it does, and as long as the American left remains incapable of national pride, our country will have only a cultural left, not a political one.

I don't believe this perception of our country could have occurred, the Vietnam war could have occurred, the acts supposedly perpetrated during that war could have occurred, if our test of validity had been right with God.

4

CONCLUSION

Three days after the present election three paragraphs from Richard Rorry's *Achieving Our Country* were tweeted:

> Members of labor unions, and unorganized unskilled workers, will sooner or later realize that their government is not even trying to prevent wages from sinking or to prevent jobs from being exported. Around the same time, they will realize that suburban white collar workers---themselves desperately afraid of being downsized---are not going to let themselves be taxed to provide social benefits for anyone else.
>
> At that point, something will crack. The non-suburban electorate will decide that the system has failed and start looking around for a strongman to vote for---

someone willing to assure them that, once he is elected, the smug bureaucrats, tricky lawyers, overpaid bond salesman, and postmodernist professors will no longer be calling the shots.

One thing that is very likely to happen is that gains made in the past forty years by black and brown Americans, and by homosexuals, will be wiped out. Jocular contempt for women will come back into fashion. All the resentment which badly educated Americans feel about having their manners dictated to them by college graduates will find an outlet.

We have elected that strongman. We must be very vigilant or we will lose our freedom. We must realize that we elected this strongman. And we need to ask the question why? I have developed a logic system which I think will get us out of this mess. I realize the average guy is not going to understand my concept of the truth or my concept of reality. He may understand that some thoughts are real and some thoughts are illusions, but he is not likely to want to understand the difference. Beliefs are incredibly powerful. Until we understand that power of beliefs, we will be subjected to a strongman like Trump.

The tweeted paragraphs above describe an electorate that is unhappy. That electorate has chosen to see happiness as their test of validity, were happiness means having status or wealth. I suggest that this is not the true meaning of happiness. I suggest that our forefathers got it right that our inalienable rights are life, liberty, and the pursuit of happiness, were happiness means being right with God. If we, as a country, want to get back to a happy environment we must be right with God. If one of our operational axioms is "I think therefore I am," then being right with God means thinking God's thoughts.

We have an example of this. An individual entered a culture where the law was the most important issue. He proceeded to challenge the spirit of that law and in doing so created enemies with those who had status or economic interest in those laws. He performed miracles consistently. And he preached a message of togetherness. The powers that be were upset to the point where they decided to kill him. Death was considered to be the end of life. This man, you probably have guessed, was named Jesus and is known as the Christ. Jesus knew that these people were going to kill him. He made no efforts at all to oppose them, they the powers that be believed they could solve their problems with violence. And they crucified him. But Jesus understood what they were trying to do and responded with love and demonstrated that death is not real. This message was so strong that it has survived for at least two thousand years. Ask any Christian today and they will tell you Christ is not dead. Jesus created the concept of eternal life. Jesus is known to have said, "I and my father are one." I think this means I think with God's thoughts and the result is eternal life.

Thinking God's thoughts means following the Holy Spirit not the ego. Thinking God's thoughts recognizes the power of loving one another. It recognizes what you do to another is done unto you. Thinking God's thoughts is a healing process that brings us together not the polarizing process of following the ego. Thinking God's thoughts does not result in a wall that symbolizes separation. The basic question that needs to be asked is can a democracy survive and not be right with God?

ABOUT THE AUTHOR

Stan McFarland is a retired engineer for the State of Ohio, who has spent his life as a seeker of truth-truth in self, in relationships, and in our culture. He currently resides in Pomeroy, Ohio, with his fifth wife on his farm with their three goats and Grand Pyrenees. Retirement has not slowed him down as he continues to use his problem-solving skills in developing new ways of generating power as he nurtures his orchard of nut-bearing trees to help increase the rural squirrel population.

His engineering and spiritual awaking started in high school when Sputnik first orbited the Earth. He became enamored with Einstein's theory of relativity and this is when Mr. McFarland developed his concept of infinite awareness. Much later in life, he was introduced to A Course in Miracles, which had a major effect on his thinking.

Mr. McFarland is a 1966 graduate of Ohio State University with a degree in mining engineering. His professional life started with management positions within the iron ore mining industry. This eventually led to him to work with the Vice President of Engineering for a major coal mining company in Shaker Heights, Ohio, before being downsized and out of work. The next decade was a struggle as he supported his family as a private land surveyor in southeast Ohio, while instructing courses at Belmont Technical College in their mining engineering curriculum. Mr. McFarland finished out his professional career as a District Test Engineer for the State of Ohio.

In his personal life, Stan has been a widower twice over and has survived two divorces leaving him with questions about just how permanent is "until death do us part?" He has two biological adult children and four adult step-children that are scattered across the country.

This book is intended to stimulate people's thinking. In particular, thought about truth, reality, and who or what is "I." the first section has what are called engineering axioms on these issues. An axiom is supposed to be self-evident. You probably heard someone say, "The truth is what I say it is." Along the same lines, Webster's dictionary defines objectives as "existing as an object or fact, independent of the mind; real," when all objects change form. Does that make objects temporarily "real"? How about this "I" business? "I am" is a powerful affirmation. It makes you whatever follows "I am." I am rich. I am sick. You can't get to either one without the use of the mind. How independent is that?

The second section is about the meaning of the words we use in our thinking. An attempt has been made to define them so that they are interrelated. For example, the traditional way the word sin is described in the religious community is missing the mark. Making a mistake "misses the mark." Does that make us sinners? Another example in the book forgiveness is described as the recognition that an act was simply an illusion and could be just let go. To do this, one must not believe the act was real. Adjusting the meaning of the words we use can have a radical effect on our actions.

The third section is about Richard Rorry's Achieving Our Country. Mr. Rorry, a philosophy professor, perceives himself as a spectator. This book was written in the hopes you will be an active participant. The book quotes Mr. Rorry extensively. Mr. Rorry uses words much differently than the book. It is hoped that when you translate the words of Mr. Rorry back into the words you think with, you will recognize you can't make our country great by yourself, as "I," but by working together "we" can.

www.ingramcontent.com/pod-product-compliance
Lightning Source LLC
LaVergne TN
LVHW020449080526
838202LV00055B/5396